Gustav Theodor Fechner

**On Life after Death**

Gustav Theodor Fechner

**On Life after Death**

ISBN/EAN: 9783337387983

Printed in Europe, USA, Canada, Australia, Japan

Cover: Foto ©Andreas Hilbeck / pixelio.de

More available books at **www.hansebooks.com**

# ON

# LIFE AFTER DEATH

FROM THE GERMAN

OF

GUSTAV THEODOR FECHNER

BY

HUGO WERNEKKE
HEAD MASTER OF WEIMAR REALSCHULE

London
SAMPSON LOW, MARSTON, SEARLE, & RIVINGTON
CROWN BUILDINGS, 188, FLEET STREET
1882

# PREFACE OF THE TRANSLATOR.

THOUGH Fechner's name is well known abroad in scientific circles, it may not be unnecessary to introduce this little book with a few remarks about himself and his writings, especially as some readers might be inclined to assume that the Professor Fechner who is eminent for his investigations on the electric forces, and on the interdependence of physical and psychical phenomena, must be a different person from the author of "Life after Death." It is by no means uncommon to find an author employed in two or more different directions, and the circumstance that his poems were published under the name of Dr. Mises, has indeed given rise to the suggestion that he wanted to keep apart Fechner the poet from Fechner the man of science. A more than superficial inspection of his writings, however, will prove this suggestion to be unfounded. It is not very difficult to trace a connexion between most, if not all, the subjects he has treated in numerous publications, both in poetry and prose, in the humorous and in the serious style.

His philosophical views are shadowed forth, though dimly and vaguely, in the humorous compositions of his early youth. The ideas laid down in the first part of his great Zend-Avesta appear as a little piece of fun in his fantasies " On the Anatomy of Angels," and the reader will be astonished to find out afterwards how very much in earnest such amusing flights of fancy may be taken, a circumstance of which the author himself was evidently not conscious at that period. These and similar productions were no doubt composed under the influence of Jean Paul Richter, who, at the time of their publication, was still alive. For Gustav Theodor Fechner began to write early.

He was born, on the 19th of April, 1801, at Gross-Särchen, a small village, on the road from Bautzen to Spremberg, in the Oberlausitz, which at present belongs to the Prussian

province of Silesia, whereas in the beginning
of our century it was under the Elector of
Saxony. It was at the ancient Saxon univer-
sity, in Leipzig, that he went through his
course of studies, and where, in 1834, he was
appointed Professor of Physics. His sphere
of activity was not confined to delivering
public lectures. He wrote and translated
science text-books, and conducted several
magazines of a scientific character. The ob-
servations preparatory to his publications on
galvanism and electro-magnetism proved
injurious to his sight, so that for some time
he was obliged to give up all writing and lec-
turing. It was, however, so far restored as
to enable him to work, most satisfactorily, in
another field, that of philosophical litera-
ture.

In 1848 he published " Nanna, or the
Soul-Life of Plants," in which he began, in a
more limited sphere, a course of investigations which soon led him from the conviction
that the organized beings inferior to man
have a soul, do not only *consist of* a body
and soul, but rather are body and soul *in one*,
like man himself, to the higher and grander

conviction that the beings superior to man, the celestial bodies, must likewise have an inward life underlying, and concomitant with, their outward life; that in fact the whole universe is alive, not a dead bulk, but an animated being, a wonderful organism of the sublimest order.

This grand doctrine was elaborately set forth in his chief work, " Zend-Avesta, on the Things of Heaven, and the Hereafter," published in 1851, in three volumes, of which the first and second contain his ideas on the relation of human life to divine life and the life of the universe, whereas the subject of the third is the relation of our present life to the life to come. The outlines of this last volume had been given, as early as 1836, in an interesting pamphlet, of a more popular character, inscribed to the two daughters of his deceased friend C. F. Grimmer, a bookseller and composer, in Leipzig.

Ever since the publication of this " Büchlein vom Leben nach dem Tode," of which the following pages would try to give the English reader a correct translation, Fechner's efforts have lain in the same direction attempting to bring about a reconciliation, so much needed in our days, of science and religion, by looking not at one side of the universe only, but diligently examining it in its two aspects, the material and the spiritual. His monistic theory (to describe it with a term which has become familiar to us of late, though generally applied, perhaps less adequately, to vastly different tenets) reminds one of the ideas proclaimed in the enthusiastic poetry and eloquent prose of Giordano Bruno, and of the views expounded, in a more pedantic form, which, in his opinion, contributed to render them all but infallible, by Benedict Spinoza. However, it is neither Brunonism nor Spinozism, nor can it be easily classed with any of the ancient or modern systems of philosophy, with almost all of which it affords interesting points of contact. By a rare combination of the poetical and the philosophical element, Fechner has accomplished to work into one system the thoughts of bygone ages and of modern thinkers, the theories of science and the doctrines of Christianity.

When Darwin's views began to attract universal attention, Fechner did neither reject, nor simply adopt them; but with a wonderful sagacity and a comprehensiveness of mind by no means frequent in a man of his age, assimilated them into his own system, giving them a new foundation, and, at the same time, deriving from them a new support to his theories. This was done in his treatise, " Some Ideas on the Creation and Evolution of Organisms " (1873).

Other publications, likewise of small extent, though of no small importance, " On the Soul-Question " (1861) and " The Three Motives and Arguments of Belief " (1863), can be barely mentioned here, as well as his series of essays on æsthetics, and his researches in physiological psychology, which became the fundament of a new science for which he proposed the name of " psychophysic " (" Elements of Psychophysic," 1860).

In " The Day-Aspect in Contrast with the Night-Aspect," published in 1879, the venerable thinker once more raised his voice against the materialist prophets of the day, a voice by no means feeble, but to which the present generation, absorbed as they are in looking at the mere outside of things, seem little inclined to listen. Perhaps it is rash and foolish to hope that this translation, undertaken, with an unpractised hand, in commemoration of Fechner's eightieth birthday, may add a few friends in England to the rather small number which up to this time he has found in his own country. If such hope should be fulfilled, this labour of love would not be quite lost. Should it, however, turn out otherwise, should the closing years of a life so honourably spent pass by without due appreciation of its work, the author's faithful disciples trust that, nevertheless, in the life hereafter, it will be granted to him to watch, enjoy, and actively promote the growth and development of the seed which he sowed in the narrow body of the present life.

H. W

WEIMAR, *November,* 1881.

# CHAPTER I.

MAN lives on earth not once, but three times : the first stage of his life is continual sleep ; the second, sleeping and waking by turns ; the third, waking for ever.

In the first stage man lives in the dark, alone ; in the second, he lives associated with, yet separated from, his fellow-men, in a light reflected from the surface of things ; in the third, his life, interwoven with the life of other spirits, is a higher life in the Highest of spirits, with the power of looking to the bottom of finite things.

In the first stage his body develops itself from its germ, working out organs for the second ; in the second stage his mind develops itself from its germ, working out organs for the third ; in the third the divine germ develops itself, which lies hidden in every human mind, to direct him, through instinct, through feeling and believing, to the world beyond, which seems so dark at present, but shall be light as day hereafter.

The act of leaving the first stage for the second we call Birth; that of leaving the second for the third, Death. Our way from the second to the third is not darker than our way from the first to the second: one way leads us forth to see the world outwardly; the other, to see it inwardly.

The infant, in the first stage, is blind and dumb to all the light and all the music of the second stage, and having to leave its mother's womb comes hard to it, and gives it pain, and at a certain moment of its birth the destruction of its former life must be like death to it, before it wakens to its new existence; in the same way we, in our present life, with all our consciousness bound up within this narrow body, know nothing of the light, the music, the freedom, and the bliss of the life to come, and often feel inclined to look upon the dark and narrow passage which leads towards it, as a little lane with "no thoroughfare" to it. Whereas death is merely a second birth into a happier life, when the spirit, breaking through his narrow hull, leaves it to decay and vanish, like the infant's hull in its first birth. And then all those things which we, with our present senses, can only know from the outside, or, as it were, from a distance, will be penetrated into, and thoroughly known, by us. Then, instead of passing by hills and meadows, instead of seeing around us all the beauties of spring, and grieving that we cannot really take them in, as they are merely external : our spirits shall enter into those hills and meadows, to feel and enjoy with them their strength and their pleasure in growing ; instead of exerting ourselves to produce, by means of words or gestures, certain ideas in the minds of our fellow-men, we shall be enabled to raise up and influence their thoughts, by an immediate intercourse of spirits, which are no longer separated, but rather brought together, by their bodies ; instead of being visible in our bodily shape to the eyes of the friends we left behind, we shall dwell in their inmost souls, a part of them, thinking and acting within them and through them.

# CHAPTER II.

THE infant, when in its mother's womb, has merely a body-spirit—the Formative Principle. Its actions are limited to growing, to producing and developing its several limbs and organs. It does not feel them as its own property, it does not use them, nor is it able to use them. A beautiful eye, a beautiful mouth are merely beautiful objects to the infant; it has produced them without being aware of their destiny, to become one day useful parts of its own self. They are made for a world to come whereof it knows nothing, worked out through some mysterious impulse, the origin of which must be traced back to the organization of its mother.[1] As soon,

---

[1] For the physiologist I would express it more distinctly, thus. The formative principle of the infant lies, before its birth, not in those parts which are to continue living after its birth, but rather in those which, in birth, must be left behind and decay, as the body of a man decays in death (placenta cum

**B**

however, as the infant, matured for the second stage of life, leaves its primary organs behind, it grows self-conscious, feels itself a self-potent individuality, endowed with creative power : the eye, the ear, the mouth henceforth are its own ; and having produced them through some innate impulse, unconsciously, it now learns to use them, rejoicing in its strength ; a world of light, of colours, sounds, odours, tastes, reveals itself through the organs produced for those purposes.

Now, the relation of the first stage of life to the second will repeat itself, in a climax, in the relation of the second stage to the third. In a similar way, as the one just alluded to, all our volitions and actions in this world are intended to produce an organism, which we shall perceive and use in the world to come as our own new Self. All the mental influences, all the effects due to the actions of a person in his lifetime, which spread all over mankind and all over the

funiculo umbilicali, velamentis ovi, eorumque liquoribus) ; thus the human being, born into the world, grows out of the infant's activity, as a continuation of it.

earth, are, even at present, bound up together by a mysterious, invisible link, thus forming a person's spiritual organs, worked out during his life and combined into a spiritual body, an organism of continually active powers and effects, of which, though indissolubly fastened to his present existence, he has no consciousness at present.

In the moment of death, however, when man has to part with those organs in which his powers of acting lay, he will, all at once, become conscious of all the ideas and effects which, produced by his manifold actions in life, will continue living and working in this world, and will form, as an organic offspring of an individual stem, an organic individuality which only then becomes alive, self-conscious, self-active, ready to act through the human and natural world, of its own will and power.

Whatever a person contributes, in his life, towards creating, transforming, or preserving the ideas pervading the human and natural world, is his own imperishable portion, able to act for itself in the third stage of life, though the body to which, during the second stage, it was inherent be long decayed. The thoughts,

actions, productions of so many millions that
are gone, are not gone with them, neither
shall they be destroyed by the thoughts,
actions, productions of many millions that
are to come ; in them and with them they
shall grow, and act, and urge them on towards
one great aim unseen by themselves.

We are inclined to look upon this ideal
continuation of our lives as a mere abstraction,
and to consider the continued influence which
the spirits of the dead exercise on the minds
of the living as an idle fantasy.  So it seems
to us, because we lack the appropriate senses
wherewith to perceive the spirits of the third
stage, in their real existence, penetrating into
the depths of the Universe : we only perceive
the ties which unite their existence with our
own, viz. those very ideas which they left
behind for us to share with them.  The circle
of waves which a falling stone produces on a
surface of water calls forth other circles round
every stone rising above the surface within
its reach ; for all that it remains one continual
circle, producing and encircling all the rest,
whereas the stones perceive it, so to speak,
only in part, as a fragment.  We are such

stones ourselves, unconscious of the encircling
waves, though, unlike those motionless stones,
we produce, every one of us, a continual circle
of actions all around us, encircling and crossing those produced by our fellow-men.

In fact, every person, in his lifetime, takes
hold of, and grows into the minds of others,
by his words and works, spoken, written, or
acted. While Goethe was still alive thousands
of cotemporaries bore within them some
sparks from the light of his genius, which
afterwards kindled up into new light. While
Napoleon was still alive, his powerful genius
exercised its influence on the whole generation almost ; and when the one and the other
died, the germs which had fallen into other
minds, did not die with them, they grew, and
developed themselves, constituting in their
total an individual being, as their origin had
been from an individual. And these new
individual beings we must assume to be pro-
vided, though in a manner incomprehensible
to us, with self-consciousness, as well in their
present state as they were before. Goethe,
Schiller, Napoleon, Luther, are still alive
among us, self-conscious individuals thinking

and acting with us, in a higher state of development now, no longer bound up within a narrow body, but pervading the world which they in their lifetime instructed, edified, delighted, ruled, and producing effects even far surpassing those of which we are generally aware.

The most striking instance of a great spirit living and working on through posterity we find in Jesus Christ. You must not think it an idle phrase, that He liveth in those who believe in Him. Every true Christian carries Him within him, not in a symbolical meaning, but in life and reality; every one that thinks and acts according to His mind has part with Him; for it is the spirit of Christ that causes in him such thinking and acting. He is diffused through all the members of His body, the Church, and they are all united through His spirit, like apples clinging to a tree, or branches attached to a vine : " For as the body is one, and hath many members, and all the members of that one body, being many, are one body : so also is Christ." (1 Cor. xii. 12.)

And like those great and this Greatest of

spirits, every true worker shall waken in the
world to come with an individuality, an organism of his own making, comprising thousands of effects and productions, filling a
narrower or wider sphere, endowed with more
or less power of growth and development,
even as their spirits in this life moved more
or less actively in their spheres of labour.
The man that has been grovelling on the
ground, employing his mental faculties only
in moving, feeding, pampering his body, will
become a very insignificant being hereafter.
The richest will then be the poorest, if he
only uses his money that he may not have to
use his powers, and the poorest may turn out
the richest, if he uses his powers to fulfil his
duties in the world. For whatever a man
uses and puts out at present will be his own
hereafter; but the pound that was kept laid
up in a napkin will be taken away entirely.

The mysteriousness of our present inward
life, the thirst after truth, which sometimes is
of but little avail here below, the desire of
every honest mind to work for the advantage
of posterity, the sense of regret and trouble
of mind caused by the consciousness of a

wicked deed, even though unaccompanied by present disadvantages, all such phenomena arise from a dim presentiment of what our fate will be hereafter, when we shall reap the fruit of our most trifling and most secret acts.

Behold in this the wonderful justice throughout the Universe, leaving it to every being to prepare for itself the conditions of its future existence. There are no outward rewards and punishments for our actions, there is no heaven or hell—in the popular meaning of the word, with Christians, Jews, and Gentiles —for the spirits of the dead to ascend or descend to, by a leap as it were ; but there is no dead stop either, no absorbing of the soul into the universe : the spirit of man has to go through his great climacteric disease, death ; after which his development will continue, in and for a higher life on this earth of ours. The foundations of that higher development, in accordance with the laws of creation, must be sought for on a lower stage ; and according as a man, in this life, has been good or bad, has acted nobly or meanly, worked hard or neglected his work, he will find, in after-life, an organism of his own, healthy or unhealthy, beautiful or ugly, strong or weak; his self-chosen way of acting in this world will determine his relation to other spirits, his faculties and talents, his whole destiny during his development in that other world.

" Let us then be up and doing ! " For he who walks at a slow pace here will be lame there ; he who opens not his eyes here will be weak-sighted there; who practises deceit and wickedness will feel at variance with all the good and faithful spirits, and that feeling will be so painful in him as to urge him on, even in the other world, to mend the evil he did in this world ; nor will he find rest and peace until his least and last offence be repaired and repented of. When other spirits rest in peace with God, partaking of His thoughts, the wicked ones will go about restless, through the sorrows and changes of earthly life, and their spiritual diseases will infect other men with error and superstition, with folly and vice ; and while they, in the third world, lag behind on the way towards perfection, they will keep back those in whom they live, on their way from the second world to the third.

Hence, meanness, wickedness, untruth, may hold their sway for a time against generosity, honesty, godliness; but in the end they will be overcome by the increasing power of the good, they will be brought to nought through their own deeds, by the increasing evil consequent thereon, and nothing shall remain in any man's spirit that is vile and impious; only what is true, good, and beautiful, is to be our eternal, imperishable portion, of which if there be but a mustard-seed in any of us (and there can be no human being utterly destitute of it), all dross and chaff which are yet around it will be taken off in the purging fire of our third life, a fire of torment for the wicked only—and in the end, be it ever so late, it will grow up into a beautiful tree.

And you, too, rejoice, whose spirit is being tried and refined here below by grief and suffering. You are only learning to be patient and persevering in removing every obstacle which would hinder your progress, and on being born into a higher life will find yourself the better enabled to make up for all it has been your lot on earth to leave undone.

# CHAPTER III.

MAN employs many means to obtain one end, God makes one means serve many ends.

The plant thinks it is here merely for its own sake, intended to grow, to wave about in the wind, to drink in light and air, to prepare colours and odours as an ornament for itself, to play with bees and butterflies. And it *is* here for its own sake, no doubt, but for the sake of the earth as well, a tiny organ of the earth for light, air, and water, to meet there and work together for the benefit of the whole terrestrial system ; it is intended to breathe for the earth, to make a verdant garment for the earth, to prepare food, raiment, and fuel, for man and beast.

Man thinks he is here merely for his own sake, intended to enjoy himself, to toil and labour for his own increase in body and mind. And he is here for his own sake, no doubt ; but his body is a dwelling-place for higher spirits as well to enter into, to commune and work together there, and thus to direct his mind to think and feel in various ways, and help him to be fit for the life to come.

Man's mind is therefore, simultaneously, his own property, and the property of those higher spirits ; and whatever comes to pass in it, belongs to both sides at once, only in a different sense and manner.

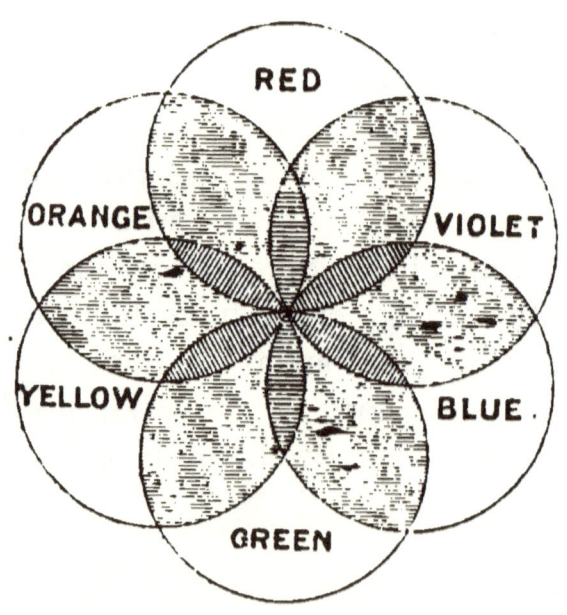

Thus, in our diagram, the many-coloured star in the middle stands for itself, an independent individual figure, whose several rays shoot from, and are kept together by a common centre; and again that same star appears to be formed by the six single-coloured circles, each of which is an independent individual figure as well, so that every ray belongs to the central star and to the intersecting circles. Behold in this not a likeness, but a symbol, of the human soul.

We often wonder whence such a thought had got into our minds; some longing, or some melancholy, or happy mood will come over us we know not how or why; an inward voice persuades us to act, or exhorts us to forbear acting, though all the time we are not conscious of any motive of our own tending one way or other. This is the influence of spirits entering into us, thinking and acting into us from centres different from our own. Such effects are the more striking in certain abnormal conditions of the mind—in som nambulism or mental distraction—when the relation of mutual dependence has been decided in *their* favour, making us entirely passive under their influence, without any reaction on our own part. As long, however, as our mind is awake and in a state of health it cannot become a mere toy, without a will of its own, of the spirits that have grown into it and become a living part of it. For such a sound human mind is an invisible life-centre of spiritual attraction, a connecting link for divers spirits, who are thus enabled to hold communion with each other, and to raise up thoughts within us. They do not, however, produce the mind, this being an inborn property of each individual person, with free-will, self-determination, self-con-sciousness, reasoning power, and all other mental faculties comprised therein. At the time of our birth, it is true, all these facul-ties are folded up as in a germ, looking forward to being developed into an organism of individual life and reality. Now, upon our entering this life those spirits draw near on all sides, trying to make use of our faculties for themselves, in order to increase their own sphere of activity, in a certain direction, and if they succeed in doing so, a new impulse in that same direction is given to our own mind in its development.

Those ingrown spirits, in their turn, are subject, though in a different way, to the in-

fluence of the human will. They influence and direct a man's mind, they also
receive new impressions from the store of
his spiritual life. In a mind harmoniously
developed, none of these influences has a
decided ascendency. For every concomitant
spirit shares only a certain part of his own
self with one individual person ; hence the
will of that person can exercise only a limited
influence on him whose sphere lies for the
greater part without him ; and as every
human mind forms a rallying-point for many
spirits, it can only be liable to a limited influence from each of them. If a man, however, of his own choice would submit entirely
to be guided by them, he would lose his con-
trol over their influences.

There are spirits opposed to each other, so
that their presence in the same human mind
is incompatible ; therefore the good and the
evil spirits, the true and the false, dispute
each other the possession of our souls. The
inward strife which we experience so fre-
quently is just such a struggle of spirits trying
to take possession of our will, our reason,
in short, our whole inward life. As a person

feels the concord of the spirits within him,
in peace, quiet, and harmony of his own self,
he also feels their strife, in inward trouble,
confusion, doubt, and despondency. But
man need not become an inert and restless
prey for the stronger spirits in that combat;
he stands, with his own active powers, in the
middle of the struggling elements who each
want to attach him to themselves ; he may, in
such strife, side with and help what party he
chooses, and may thus decide the victory even
in favour of the weaker side, adding his own
powers to those of the spirit against the stronger
ones. Thus his individuality, his own self, will
remain unshaken as long as he preserves his
inborn power and freedom, never tiring to use
them. If, nevertheless, he is led on by evil
spirits, it is from the difficulty he may find
in using his own inward strength : thus, to become bad, it is enough to be idle and careless.

The better a man's character is, the more
easy it will be for him to go on improving ;
and the worse he is, the more easily he will
turn utterly bad. For a good man has received many good spirits within himself, who,
uniting their powers with his, will save him

some effort in getting rid of the evil spirits that have remained in him or approach him. Therefore, doing good is no trouble for a good man; he has his good spirits to help him, whereas a wicked man, to follow any good intentions he may have formed, must first overcome, by his own efforts, the evil spirits that resist his intentions.

Besides, kindred spirits will find, and associate with, each other, flying from contrary ones, if not forced to stay. The good spirits within us call other good spirits around us, and the evil spirits within us attract the evil ones. Pure spirits rejoice to come and live in a pure mind, but outward evil takes hold of the evil within us. If good spirits in increasing numbers take their abode in our soul, the last devil that had lingered there will soon flee away, they are no fit company for him; and thus the soul of the good man becomes a pure heavenly dwelling for blessed spirits, abiding there in sweet company. Again, good spirits when they see the impossibility of reclaiming a soul from the predominant evil ones, leave it all to them, and it becomes a hell, a place full of the tor-

ment of the damned.   For the pangs of con-
science, and the trouble and restlessness in
the minds of the wicked are torments not
only felt by themselves, but by the evil spirits
within them as well, even with more intensity.

## CHAPTER IV.

THE higher spirits, living as they are not in a single person, but each living and acting in more than one, are a spiritual link between those persons, uniting them all in the same belief, the same truth, the same moral or political tendency. All the persons having a certain spiritual interest between them, belong to the body of one spirit, and as co-ordinate members of it, work out the ideas which they have received from that spirit. Sometimes an idea lives in a whole nation, a multitude of people are roused up to one great common enterprise : here is a mighty spirit coming over them all, penetrating them all. Such universal influences, however, are not only brought about by the spirits of the dead; also numberless new-born ideas of the living influence those living around them; but all the ideas which a living person sends forth into the world are also elements and members of his future spiritual organism.

Now, wherever two kindred spirits meet on earth, growing into one through their common qualities, and influencing and enriching one another through their different qualities, the communities, nations, or generations, to which they formerly belonged individually, enter into spiritual communion as well, increasing thereby the mental stores and powers of each other. Thus the development of spiritual life in the third stage is closely connected with the development and progress of mankind. The gradual formation and growth of states, the progress of science and art, of commerce and trade, the development of all these spheres into larger and larger bodies harmoniously organized, is the consequence of numberless spirits living and moving among men and growing together into more extended spiritual organisms. How could it be possible for all those important spheres of life to take shape on great immutable principles, if they were to rely on the confused selfish actions of individuals too short-sighted to see from the centre to

the circumference, or from the circumference
to the centre? How could it be possible,
were not this activity influenced by higher
spirits, who see clearly through the whole
system, and, crowding round the common
divine centre, and flowing together with
their divine elements, direct men, between
them, towards higher aims.

But as there is a harmony of spirits kindly
meeting and helping each other, so is there
also a strife of spirits, in which all earthly
and finite concerns must in the end destroy
one another, leaving the things eternal alone
in their purity. Symptoms of this struggle
may also be observed in the human world, in
the antagonism of systems, the hatred of
parties, the wars and rebellions between
sovereigns and nations.

The majority of men stand amid these
great spiritual movements, with blind faith,
blind obedience, blind hatred and fury,
neither hearing with their own ears nor
seeing with their own eyes, but directed by
other spirits towards ends and aims of which
they know nothing, allowing themselves to
be led on through misery, slavery, and death,

following the impulse of those higher spirits like a herd of cattle.

On the other side, there are men who, both acting and directing, influence the movement with clear consciousness and inward independence. But, after all, they are only voluntary instruments for bringing on great predisposed effects, whose free actions may indeed determine the way and rate of the progress, but not its end and object. Those men who have accomplished great things in the world, were enabled to do so by their insight into the spiritual tendency of the period in which they lived, and they succeeded by making their free acting and thinking agree with that tendency, while other men, perhaps just as great and sincere, failed, because opposing that tendency. That first class of men were chosen by the Spirit who knows what ways are best to what ends, to be new centres for his moving powers, not in the manner of blind tools, but of living instruments serving his wisdom and justice, of their own free-will and with their own powers of intellect. It is not the slave under the taskmaster that does the better work.　And what they begin to work in the service of God beneath they will continue hereafter, when they are partakers of His heavenly kingdom.

# CHAPTER V.

On many occasions when the spirits of the living and the dead meet, they may both be unconscious of the meeting; or the consciousness may be on one side only—who is there that could follow or fathom such intercourse! So let it be understood that, whenever we speak of their meeting each other, we mean that they meet consciously, and whenever we speak of the presence of the dead, we mean that they are present consciously.

There is one means of meeting consciously for the living and the dead: it is in the memory of the living for the dead. To direct our attention to the dead is to attract their attention towards us, just as an outward impression on a living person will direct his attention to the place where it acts upon him.

Our memory of the dead is indeed nothing

but a consequence of their own conscious life beneath ; a consequence brought to our consciousness ; but their whole life in the hereafter is made up of the consequences of their present life.

Our thinking of a living person may very well cause some influence on his mind; but it is of no effect, as his consciousness is held within the bonds of his earthly frame. But consciousness set free by death seeks its own place, yielding to the influences exercised upon it the more easily and decidedly, the more easily and decidedly those influences have been exercised before.

One material stroke is always felt double, by him that strikes and by him that is struck : so one stroke of consciousness, produced by thinking of a dead person, is connected with a double sensation. We are mistaken if we only think of the share which our present life has in that mental act, unmindful of the share of the life hereafter : a mistake and neglect which cannot remain without their consequences.

If a lover has lost his beloved one, a husband his wife, a child its mother, it is in

vain for them to look to distant heavens for
the piece torn off their own lives, straining
their eyes and stretching out their hands into
vacancy for that which has never been really
torn away from them; it is only the thread
of bodily communication that is broken;
the intercourse through their outward senses,
whereby they both understood each other,
has given way to an immediate connexion
through their inward senses, which they have
not learnt yet to understand.

I saw a mother once looking anxiously
about the house and garden for her own
living child which all the time she was carry-
ing in her arms. A greater error than hers
is the error of her who will look for her dead
child in some distant space, whereas it would
suffice to look into her own self to find it.
And if she does not find it there entire,
was it entire, was it all her own, strictly
speaking, when she carried it outwardly in
her arms? It is true, the advantages of
outward intercourse, of outward words,
looks, and care-taking are lost to both; the
advantages of an inward intercourse have
only begun now, if she only knows that

there is such an inward intercourse and sees the advantages it has. Nobody will speak to or shake hands with a person whom he supposes to be absent; but if you once know better, and have learnt to see in a clearer light, there will be for you a new life of the living with their dead, and the dead will profit by this knowledge no less than the living.

If you think of a dead person earnestly and intensely, not only the thought of him or her, but the dead person himself will be in your mind immediately. You may inwardly conjure him, he must come to you; you may hold him, he must stay with you, if you only fix your thoughts upon him. Think of him in love or in hatred, he will be sure to feel it; think of him with strong love, with stronger hatred, he will feel it the more strongly. Up to this you have had your memories of the dead, now you know the use of them, henceforth you will be able at will to make a dead person happy or miserable, through thinking of him, to reconcile yourself to him or quarrel with him, consciously for him as well as for yourself. Do so, then, but always for a good purpose, and take care that the memory which you leave behind one day may be to your own advantage.

Blessed the man who left behind him a store of love, of respect, and veneration, in the memory of men. What he left behind in his present life he will gain in his death, acquiring a comprehensive consciousness of all that is thought of him by those who remain behind; he will thus carry home the bushel of which he had but single grains to count in his lifetime. Here is part of the treasure which we are bidden to lay up for heaven.

Woe to the man whom curses and execrations, a memory of terror, follow! What followed him in this life will overtake him in death: here is part of the hell that awaits him. Each cry of misery that is sent after him will turn out a sharp arrow reaching him to pierce his very heart.

Full justice is done to every man: it consists in the totality of the consequences of both his good and evil actions. The good man who was misjudged here must suffer from that circumstance for some time, hereafter, as from an outward evil; and his false glory will follow the unjust man as an outward good; therefore, it will be well for you to keep your reputation clean and not to hide your light under a bushel. But among the spirits hereafter there will be no misjudging; what was weighed amiss here will be set right above, and will be over-weighed by an addition to the other side of the balance. For heavenly justice shall finally overcome all injustice of the earth.

Whatever wakens the memory of the dead is a means of calling them to our side. At every festival arranged to commemorate them, they rise; round every statue which we erect in their honour, they float; to every song celebrating their noble acts, they listen. Here is a vital germ for a new phase of art ! Art has grown so old, so tired of repeating old spectacles before the old lookers-on again and again; here is another tier of boxes opening, as it were, above the pit filled with the old spectators ; now we know of a company of a higher class looking down from above, and the noblest object of art will be, henceforth, to please those above, no longer those below; but the people below ought to be pleased with that which is approved of above.

The scoffers go on scoffing, and the churches continue quarrelling—scoffing and quarrelling about a mystery which the scoffers say is repugnant to reason, and which the churches declare is above reason; for a greater secret has remained concealed from both parties, the opening of which removes at last, in a very simple and easy manner, the difficulty which defied the reason of scoffers and disturbed the harmony of the churches; it is simply the greatest illustration of an universal rule, wherein they would see an exception from every rule or something above all rule. It is not in a mere body of flour and water that Christ is received by the faithful partaker of His holy Supper. If you receive it in the thought of Him, He is with His thoughts not only near you, but within you; the more earnestly you think of Him the more closely He will unite Himself with you. But if you do not think of Him at all. you eat and drink nothing but common bread and common wine.

## CHAPTER VI.

THE natural desire of every man to be, after his death, once more united with those he loved most dearly in this life, shall be fulfilled in a more perfect degree than you ever thought of or hoped for.

Those who were united in their life by a mutual spiritual element shall, in the hereafter, not only meet, but grow into one, through that very element which shall become a mutual organ of their spirits, of which they both partake with equal consciousness. For even now the dead and the living, as well as the living among each other, are grown into one by numberless elements of that kind, elements which they have in common ; but not till death has undone the bonds in which this frame of ours holds every soul of the living will the connexion of their consciousness be enhanced into a consciousness of their connexion. In

the moment of death every one will realize
the fact that what his mind received from
those who died before him, never ceased to
belong to their minds as well, and thus he
will enter the third world not like a strange
visitor, but like a long expected member of
the family, who is welcomed home by all
those with whom he was before connected in
the community of faith, of knowledge, or of
love.

We shall also enter into close communion
with the great spirits of those who lived, in
their second stage of life, long before us,
but whose great example and wisdom served
to form our own minds.   Thus he who lived
here entirely in Christ will be entirely in
Christ hereafter ; nor is his individuality to
be destroyed within a higher individuality ;
nay, he will be established, and receive new
strength, and will be able to strengthen
others at the same time.   For such spirits as
are grown into one by their common elements must profit of each other's strength,
while, at the same time, they influence each
other through their different elements. Some
spirits will strengthen each other in many

parts of their character, while others have only few points of coincidence and of mutual interest; some of these connexions brought about by the kindred elements in different spirits may be dissolved again, but those whose tendency is towards truth, virtue, and beauty will continue.

All things which have no elements of eternal harmony in them, though continuing beyond this life, must one day vanish away, thereby separating those spirits who for some time were united in a blamable connexion, working for no good.

Though the different elements of human spirits contain, for the greater part, some germ of the true, the beautiful, and the good, that germ is, in this life, covered up and encumbered with much that is trifling, ugly, false, and wrong. The spirits united by such elements may, in after-life, either remain united or not : for they may either hold what is right and good, leaving that which is wrong and wicked to the evil spirits whose company they shun; or some of them may keep the good, others the bad, elements.

On the contrary, spirits united by their

D

mutual possession of some element or idea of the true, the beautiful, or the good, in its eternal purity, will remain united for ever, sharing for ever the same spiritual property.

In the same measure, therefore, as the higher spirits comprehend the eternal ideas, they will grow together in larger spiritual organisms; and as the roots of all individual ideas are in general ideas, and theirs again in more general and universal ideas, all the spirits will, in the end, be united—in wonderful organization—with the greatest of spirits, with God.

Thus the spiritual world, in its perfection, is not a simple gathering together of spirits, but it may be likened to a living tree of spirits, with its roots in the earth and its crown reaching throughout the heavens.

The greatest and noblest spirits only are able to penetrate immediately to the inward height and greatness of God; the smaller and minor spirits grow into them as twigs into branches, and branches into trees, connected, through their mediation, with the highest essence of the most High.

Dead geniuses and saints (or Heroes, as

Carlyle would call them) are, therefore, the true mediators between God and men, partaking, on one side, of the ideas of God and communicating them to men, and feeling, on the other side, the joys and sufferings of mankind and communicating them to God.

In the very beginnings of religious life the worship of the dead was closely connected with the worship of deified nature ; the savage races have retained the greater, the civilized races the higher part of those views, and there is no people or community that do not hold more or less of them as a principal article of faith.   Therefore, every town ought to erect a temple for their own great dead, which might be built close by, or right into, the temple of God, whereas Christ alone ought to be always worshipped in the same place with God.

# CHAPTER VII.

"Now we see through a glass, darkly ; but then face
to face ; now I know in part ; but then shall I know
even as also I am known." 1 Cor. xiii. 12.

MAN leads both an outward and an inward life in this world ; the one visible and
perceptible for every one in his looks, words,
works, and deeds ; the other perceptible only
for himself in his thoughts and emotions.
The continuation of the visible life into the
world around may be easily traced, the continuation of the invisible life remains invisible, but is by no means wanting. For as
man's inward life forms the centre of his
present existence, its continuation will form
the centre of his future existence.

Indeed, the effects which a person produces in a form visible and palpable for the
living, are not the only emanation from him.
However minute and gentle a vibration con-

nected with some conscious movement within our mind may be—and all our mental acts are connected with, and accompanied by, such vibrations of our brain—it cannot vanish without producing continued processes of a similar nature, within ourselves, and, finally, around ourselves, though we are not able to trace them into the outer world. A lyre cannot keep its music for itself; as little can our brain; the music of sounds or of thoughts originates in the lyre or in the brain, but does not stay there—it spreads beyond them.

What a wonderfully complicated play of vibrations of a higher order, originating in our brain, may be going on along with the coarser and lower play that strikes our eyes and ears, something like the most delicate ripple on the top of the big waves in a lake, or the finely traced ornaments on the surface of a carpet, which receives its whole value and higher meaning from them. The man of science only knows and studies the play of waves of a lower order, little caring for those of a higher order. He does not perceive them, but knowing the principle, he ought not to neglect the inferences that may be derived from it.[1]

Therefore, the effects produced by any human spirit are not limited to his continued influence by means of his outward life in the present stage : along with this outer part there is in our nature another, inner, part, even the essential part of the human being. Suppose a man to have lived and died in some desert island without any direct influence on another man's life : he must continue in his individuality, in expectance of future development, having been unable to develop himself in this life through intercourse with his fellow-men. In the same way a child, which has been alive only for a moment, can

[1] The play of the nerves may be reduced to chemical or electrical processes. In either case it must be acknowledged either to consist of the vibrations of ultimate particles, or at least to be evoked by or connected with them, though the imponderable substance may herein be of greater moment than the ponderable. Now vibrations can only *seem* to die out, in so far as they spread indefinitely in all directions ; or, if dying out for a time, transformed into energy or tension, they are able to begin afresh, in some form or other, in accordance with the law of the conservation of energy.

never die again. The shortest moment of conscious life produces a circle of actions around it, just as the briefest tone that seems gone in a second, produces a similar circle, which carries the tone into endless space, far beyond the persons standing by to listen; for no action, or effect, is utterly destroyed, it goes on producing new effects of its kind for ever. Thus the mind of the child will develop itself from that one conscious moment, as well as the mind of that isolated man, but in a different way from what it would have done when beginning from a more developed state.

It is only in death that a man becomes fully conscious of all the influence he exercised on other men's minds; in the same way it will be only in death that he enters into full possession and use of what he produced within himself. What mental treasures he gathered in, all his life, what fills his memory, what pervades his feelings, what his mind and fancy created, is to remain his property for ever. The connexion and interdependence of all these mental stores remains a mystery for us in this life. Thoughts will occasionally pass through this treasure-house, lighting up with their rays the little corner that lies on their way, leaving the rest in darkness. Our mind never knows its whole internal store at once ; detached ideas only, happening to find a new idea to associate with, rise out of the dark for a moment, to return into dark the next moment. Thus man is a stranger to his own mind, in which he gropes in the dark, trusting to his syllogisms to guide him, and often forgetting the best of his treasures, which happen to lie out of his way concealed by the darkness spread over the regions of the human spirit. In the moment of death, however, when eternal night sinks down on his bodily eyes, a new day will break upon his spirit ; the centre of the inner man will flame up into a sun, which sheds its radiance over all his spiritual stores, and at the same time penetrates into and looks through them as an inward eye of unearthly keenness. All the things that had gone out of his mind in this life, man will then find again ; they only dropped from his mind, as *they* went to the hereafter before him, where he finds them all gathered up for him, in a

new and universal light, which saves him the
trouble of collecting what he wants to associate, and dividing what he wants to separate. At a glance he will be able to survey
all that is in him, his various ideas in their
relations of agreement and contradiction, of
connexion and separation—not confined to
one particular direction of his thoughts, but
looking into every direction at once. There
are instances of persons approaching such a
state of inward illumination, even in this life,
in cases of approaching death, as by drown-
ing, or in somnambulism, or narcosis, and
such like.

As high as the flight and sight of a bird
mount above the lowly path of the blind
and crawling caterpillar, that knows nothing
but what it touches in its slow movements,
so that higher state of knowledge will far
surpass our present state. So that in death
not only our body, but our senses, our intellect, the whole constitution of our mind,
must be cast off, as forms too narrow for our
life hereafter, as useless members for the new
order of things, where everything that we
could approach and investigate but slowly

and imperfectly with such earthly organs, will be immediately within ourselves, for us to look through, and know, and enjoy it. Every man's own self, however, in the middle of that destruction of temporary forms, will remain unimpaired in its whole extent and development, and there will be for him a new and higher life instead of the inferior kind of activity which has been extinguished. The turmoil of thoughts is hushed, they need no longer come and go, and move about, to become conscious of their relation to each other. Instead of the intercourse of thoughts, a higher intercourse, between spirits and spirits, will begin. And as the intercourse of human thoughts takes place in a human spirit, so the intercourse and communion of spirits will take place in that higher spirit whose all-connecting centre we call God. For them no language is required to understand, no eye to see and recognize, each other. Just as one thought of ours understands and influences another without the mediation of mouth, ear, or hand; as thoughts meet and part without an outward link or separation ; so secret, close, and immediate

will the communion of spirits be. There is
nothing those spirits will be able to conceal from
each other; every sinful thought that lurked
here in some dark corner of the mind, everything a man would like to cover up from his
fellow-men with a thousand hands, will be
clear and open to every spirit. Only such
spirits, therefore, as were all pure and true
in this life, will be able to meet other spirits
unashamed hereafter; and such as were set
aside and misjudged here will be understood
and appreciated hereafter. Again, every
spirit with a self-penetrating eye will perceive
all his own defects, and whatever he left, in
this life, unfinished, imperfect, and discordant
within himself, and perceiving these defects
will feel them with the same keenness of sensation with which we feel our bodily defects.
And as in the human mind one thought
helps to free the other from all that is untrue
in it, and as they associate into higher
thoughts, supplying in this wise what is de-
fective and imperfect in each of them : just
so the communion of spirits will serve them
as a means for their progress towards perfection.

## CHAPTER VIII.

MAN'S intercourse with nature, in this life, is of a material as well as of a spiritual kind. Heat, air, water, earth enter into and issue from him in every direction, forming and changing his body. Around him, they move alongside of each other, within him they meet and combine, and in their combination make up a frame, which shuts off his bodily sensations and whatever there is still deeper than these within him, from immediate contact with the outer world. Thus he looks and feels into the outer world through the windows of his senses, and draws fragmentary knowledge out of it as in little buckets.

After his death, however, when his bodily frame sinks into decay, the spirit, fettered and encumbered no longer, will roam throughout nature in unbound liberty.[1] Then he will feel

---

[1] The translator was struck with an illustration of this view, contained in a letter of Chas. Dickens to his

the waves of light and sound not only as they strike his eyes and ears, but as they glide along in the oceans of air and of ether; he will feel not only the breathing of the wind and the heaving of the sea against his body bathing in them, but float along through air and sea himself; he will no longer walk among verdant trees and fragrant meadows, but consciously penetrate the fields, and forests, and men as they walk about them.

Thus, what he loses in passing to a higher stage of life are nothing but organs the imperfect aid of which he may gladly dispense with in a state of existence where he shall feel, and perfectly and actually take in, everything that, on a lower stage, lay outside his own self and could not be approached but by the slow mediums before mentioned.

friend J. Forster (The Life of C. D., chap. xxxiii.):—
" What would I give if you and Mac were here [by the side of Niagara], to share the sensations of this time ! I was going to add, what would I give if the dear girl whose ashes lie in Kensal Green, had lived to come so far along with us—but she has been here many times, I doubt not, since her sweet face faded from my earthly sight."

Why should we take our eyes and ears with us into the life to come, to draw in light and sound from living nature's well, as the waves of that life shall move in harmony and union with the very waves of light and sound ? Nay more : The human eye, though kindred to the sun, is but a tiny thing, perceiving of the glory of the skies but little sparkling dots. Man's wish to know more of the heavens remains unfulfilled in this life. Though he invent telescopes to enlarge the power and capacity of his eyes, it is in vain—the stars are only so many dots for him. So he hopes to obtain in the life to come what his present life cannot afford him, he trusts to have his longings satisfied when he shall go to heaven, and to see, henceforth, distinctly everything that was hidden from his earthly sight. And he is right in hoping so, though he shall not receive wings to go to heaven and fly from star to star with, or from the heavens visible above us to higher heavens yet unseen ; there are no such wings in the nature of things. Nor is he to see the heavens in being carried from one star to another in a succession of new births ; there

are no storks to carry babies from star to
star.[1]  Nor will his eye receive more visual
power to penetrate into the farthest distances
of heaven, by being turned into the largest
kind of telescope ; the principle of our earthly
vision would prove insufficient there.  When,
as a conscious part of the great celestial body
that carries and holds him—the Earth—he
consciously partakes in the intercourse, through
light, between this and other heavenly beings:
then shall he see his longings satisfied.  What,
a new kind of sight?  Well, it would not be
fit for men below, just as our present sight
would not suffice for the heavens above.[2]
Through heavenly space the Earth floats
along, an enormous eye, immersed in an
ocean of the light which proceeds from
numberless stars, and wheeling round and

[1] Perhaps it will not be unnecessary to explain, for
the English reader, that, from time immemorial, the
children in Germany have firmly believed that their
little brothers and sisters are laid into their cradles by
the stork that fetches them from some mysterious well
in Fairyland.   [Translator's Note.]

[2] Lest this assumption, apparently involving serious
difficulties, might be considered thoughtless, I shall
more fully explain the meaning of it in an appendix.

round to receive, on all sides, the impact of its waves, which cross and cross again, a million of times, without ever disturbing each other.   It is with that eye man shall learn to see one day, to look into heaven, meeting with the spreading waves of his future life the outward waves of the surrounding ether, and penetrating, with its most subtle vibrations, undisturbed by the encountering waves, into the depths of heaven.

Learn to see, indeed!   A great many things man will have to learn after his death.   For you must not expect that you shall take in, on your very entrance into it, the whole splendour of heaven, which is in store for the life to come.   In this life a child must learn to see and hear; what it sees and hears in the beginning are sights and sounds meaningless for it, dazzling, stunning, confusing.   The same will be the case, in the life to come, with what is offered to the new senses of the new child.   Only what man takes away with him of this life, the remembrance of all he did, thought, and was, he will see clearly and distinctly within him, as soon as he enters that new life : but this evidently leaves him very much the same man he was before. And you may be sure that the foolish, the idle, the wicked shall profit of the glory of the hereafter only so far as they are made to see the discord of their being, and are compelled, in the end, to give up their old evil ways. Even for his present life man has received an eye to see all the marvels of heaven and earth, an ear to drink in the sounds of music and of human speech, a mind to take in the meaning of all these things— yet, what is the use of eye, ear, or mind to the foolish, the idle, the wicked ?

The best and highest things of the life to come, as well as of the present life, are only for the best and highest men, who alone understand, appreciate, attempt, and help to produce, them. Thus only the higher class of spirits will be enabled to understand, and take an active part in, the conscious intercourse of the celestial being that carries them with other beings of the "company of heaven."

Whether, after æons of years, this earth of ours, revolving round the sun in closer and closer orbits, shall return to the womb

E

whence it issued, for a new, solar life to commence for all earthly creatures—who knows? And would it behove us to know, at present?

# CHAPTER IX.

THE spirits of the third stage dwell in the regions of this Earth, whereof mankind itself forms a part, as in a common body, and to them all the processes in nature are the same as the processes in our bodies are to us at present. Their body encloses the bodies of the second stage of life as a common mother, just as the bodies of the second stage enclose those of the first.

But for every spirit of the third stage only that part of their common body which he contributed to form and develop during his earthly life, will be his own. Whatever in this world has become, through the existence of a certain human being, different from what it would have been without him, helps to constitute his new existence, grown out of the common root of all existence, and made up, partly of solid institutions and works, partly

E 2

of moving and spreading effects, in a similar way as our present body is made up of solid material, and of changeable material kept together by the solid.

Now, as the spheres of existence wherein the lives of higher spirits move must necessarily interfere, the question arises how it is possible for such numberless spheres to cross and recross each other without disturbing and confusing each other. But you may as well ask how it is possible for numberless water waves to cross in the same lake, for numberless air waves to cross in the same atmosphere, for numberless waves of light to cross in the same ether, for numberless waves of memory to cross in the same brain, for numberless spheres of human lives—the germs and substructions of their after-lives—to cross in this world without disturbing and confusing each other. On the contrary, they only produce a movement and life, of a higher order, of those waves, those memories, those lives of the second, and also of the third stage.

But what is there that keeps those crossing spheres of consciousness asunder? Nothing

is there to keep them asunder in any particular points of coincidence, for they all
have their points in common, though they
belong to each of them in a different manner:
this is what separates them and distinguishes
them as individuals. Or would you ask
what there is to distinguish or separate the
interfering circles of waves? You are able to
distinguish them outwardly, though they are
all alike; and it must be much easier for
spheres of consciousness to distinguish each
other and themselves inwardly.

When you get a letter from India or Australia having its pages crossed with writing in
different directions, how do you manage to
distinguish the two sets of lines? Simply by
the inward connexion of each set. Now, the
world may be compared to such a sheet
crossed with divers sets of writing, in ever so
many directions, every set reading itself as it
stands by itself, and reading as well the other
sets by which it is crossed. But that letter
is only a very imperfect image of the world.

How, then, can consciousness remain one,
when spread over such an extended space?
Is there not the law about "the Threshold

of Consciousness "? [1]   You may as well ask
how can it remain one in the more limited
space of your body, of which that more extended space is only a continuation.   Your
body, your brain, are they mere points?   Or
is there one particular point in them, the seat
of the soul?   There is no such point.   The
function, nay the essence of your soul at present is to keep up the connexion of all the
parts of your small body ; hereafter it will be,
to keep up the more extensive connexion of
all the parts of your larger body.   The spirit
of God keeps up the connexion of the whole
Universe, and would you look for God in a

---

[1] This empirical law of the reciprocity of body and
mind states, that consciousness is extinguished whenever the bodily activity on which it is dependant, sinks
below a certain degree of power, called the Threshold.
The more extended this activity, the more it will be
weakened, and the more easily it will sink below the
threshold.   There is such a threshold for our consciousness as a whole—the limit between sleeping and
waking—and a particular one for every particular
sphere of the mind.   Hence, in the waking state, the
one or the other idea will rise or sink in our mind,
according as the particular activity on which it depends
rises above, or sinks below, its respective threshold.

point? And one day you shall more fully partake of His ubiquity.

Or, if you are afraid that the waves of your future life may be too extended to rise to the threshold which they reach and overstep in this life, you ought to consider that, far from spreading into an empty world where they would indeed sink into an abyss, they spread into a world, which, as the eternal foundation for the spirit of God, will be a foundation for yours as well : for it is only as supported by and enclosed in the life of God that any creature can live.

The little wren, supported on the eagle's back, flies high above the summits of the mountains, which she could never do for herself; she can even soar a little higher, above the eagle's back where it rested. But both eagle and wren remain in the care of God.

Another question arises—how, after death, we shall be able to exist without our brain, that wonderful work of art, which at present supports all our mental activity, developing itself in the same measure as that activity grows and develops itself—was it given to us for no purpose? It would be the same question, how the plant can exist without the seed out of which it bursts forth into life, growing up towards the light : the seed, which is such a wonderful work of art, developing itself more and more through its own vitality ; was that seed made for no purpose ?

Now you ask where there is, in all the world around us, another structure as wonderful as the human brain, that might take its place in after-life, or where there is any structure even superior to it : for the life to come is supposed, justly, to be superior to the present life. But is not your body, as a whole, a larger and grander structure than your eye, your ear, your brain, or any of its parts ? And the world of which mankind, with their commonwealths, their sciences, arts, and commerce form only a part, is again, in the same degree, nay in an unutterably higher degree, superior to your little brain, which is only a part or particle of that part. To obtain a higher view of the subject, you must not take the earth for a mere ball of land and water and air ; the earth is indeed a larger and higher individual creature than

yourself, a heavenly being, with a more wonderful living and moving on its surface than
you carry about in your own little brain, con-
tributing thereby your own small share of
terrestrial life. It is vain for you to dream
of a life to come, before you have learned to
see the life which is actually around you.

What does the anatomist behold in a man's
brain? It is to him a labyrinth of whitish
strings, the meaning of which he cannot read.
And what does the brain see in itself? A
world of light, and sound, and thoughts,
associations, fancies, emotions of love and
hatred. From this circumstance you may
form an idea of the difference between that
which you see of the world, looking at it from
the outward, and that which the world sees
within itself. Then you will no longer expect
that in the world as a whole the inward and
outward ought to resemble one another more
than in the case of yourself, as a part of the
world. And only from being a part of the
world you are enabled to see within yourself
a part of that which the world sees in itself.

Finally, you may ask what it is that in
after-life, and not till then, wakens our larger

body, so to speak. For that body exists at present, growing and spreading into the outer world as a continuation of our present narrow body. Well, it wakens from the very fact that this narrow body falls asleep, or rather decays. It is only a particular case of the universal rule, which holds good for all this present life, whence we conclude that it will hold good hereafter. In your sceptic way, you insist on drawing all your conclusions from this life ; so you ought to draw this one also.

Conscious energy is in fact never produced afresh, nor can it be absolutely destroyed. Similar to the body with which it is connected, it may change its place, form, and activity, in time and space. When it sinks to-day in one place, it will rise in another place to-morrow. That your eye may be awake, may *see* consciously, your ear must go to sleep for a while ; that your mental activity may be roused, your senses must sleep for a while ; a feeling of pain in some minute part of your body may for a time extinguish all your consciousness. When directed to a large range of subjects at once, the light of attention must shine but feebly into the details ; when concentrated on a certain point, all the rest recede into darkness ; to reflect on something is to abstract from other things. You are awake to-day because you slept yesterday, and the more active you have been in waking, the sounder will be your sleep.

Now, in this life, our sleep, in a certain sense, is only half-sleep, allowing the old man to waken again, because the old man is still here ; in death our sleep will be full sleep, out of which shall waken a new man, for the old man is not : but the old rule holds good again, requiring some substitute for your old consciousness ; and as there is a new body instead of the old one, being a continuation of the same, so there will be a new consciousness, as a substitute and continuation of the old one.

A continuation, I say ; for whatever preserves, in the aged man, the consciousness that dwelled in the body of the child, of which not an atom is left in his body, will preserve, in his future life, the same consciousness that dwelled in the body of the aged man, of which not an atom will be left in the new body. For in either case the new body comprehends and preserves the effects of the former body, the organ of his former consciousness, and is itself the outgrowth of it. Thus there is one principle for the continuation of our present life, from this day to the morrow, and for the continuation of the present life into the life to come. And could there be any principle but an eternal one for the eternal continuation of human life?

As little need you ask, how it is that the effects wrought by you in this world, which have spread around and beyond yourself, belong to you more properly and more closely than any other effects lying beyond your sphere. The reason for this is in their origin from you. Every cause keeps its effects as an eternal property. And, after all, your acts never went beyond yourself, forming as they do, in this life, an unconscious continuance of yourself, and looking forward to being wakened into new consciousness.

As little as a human being, when once alive, can ever die again, as little could it have wakened into life had it not been alive before; only it was not alive individually. The consciousness which wakens in a child at its birth is only part of the eternal and universal consciousness coming to take its abode in this new soul. The difficulty is to trace this living consciousness through all its ways and changes, just the same difficulty as with the living bodily powers.

Perhaps you are afraid that human consciousness, being born of the universal consciousness, may be again absorbed into the same. Behold the tree! What a time it took for the stem to grow branches; but once here they cannot be swallowed up into the stem again, else the tree could not grow and develop itself: but the tree of universal life must grow and develop itself as well.

After all, to draw any conclusion from this life about the hereafter, we must not take our stand on unknown causes or self-made premises; but on known facts, from whence to proceed to the greater and higher facts of after-life, and thus to strengthen and support our belief from below, in addition to higher arguments, and vitally to connect this belief with practical life. Were it not an inward want, we should require no support for it; but without such support, how should we meet that want?

## CHAPTER X.

THE human soul is spread throughout the body; when the soul departs the body decays. The consciousness of the soul is in different places at different times.[1] We saw it wandering about in our narrow body, now corresponding with the eye, now with the ear, with the outer and inner senses; in death, it will wander beyond our body, like a man who, having had his little house destroyed wherein he moved about for years, leaves it

[1] Or, to express it more exactly, consciousness is present and awake when and where the activity of the body underlying the activity of the mind—the psycho-physical activity—is raised beyond the degree which we call the threshold. According to this view, consciousness may be localized in time and space. The summits of the waves of our psycho-physical activity move and change about from place to place, though confined, in this life, to our body, even to a limited part of our body. In sleep they sink below the threshold to rise again in waking.

for ever to wander to remote countries. Death separates our two lives only so far as it takes us from the narrow scene of our wanderings to a wider one. Now, in this life consciousness cannot be in all places at once ; the same in after-life. But the range of its wanderings will be incomparably wider, with freer roads, with higher points of view, comprehending all the lower ones of the present life.

Even in this life it may happen, though very rarely, that consciousness wanders from the narrow body into the larger body, and returning home gives information about things which are taking place far away in space, or things which, springing from present circumstances, will take place in some future time : for the length of the future rests on the breadth of the present. Sometimes a little chink does open, suddenly, and quickly close again, in the gate, generally shut up, between this world and the next, the gate which only death is to open for good and ever. Nor is it well for us to peep through those chinks before the time. But such exceptions from the rule of our present life are still in harmony with the greater rule which comprehends both this life and the life hereafter.

The narrower body falls asleep to a certain extent, in an uncommon way, wakening in a no less uncommon way, in another direction, beyond its usual limits, though only for a short period. Or, some part of our larger body is impressed with such uncommon intensity as to draw our consciousness, for a while, away from our narrower body, to rise above the threshold in an unusual place. Hence the wonders of second sight, of forebodings and dreams—mere fables, if our future body and our future life are fables, otherwise signs of the one and harbingers of the other : and if a thing has its signs, it must have existence ; if it has its harbingers, it will come on.

However, all those things are no signs of a healthy life. For in this life we have only to work out our bodies for the hereafter, not to see or hear with the eyes and ears of the hereafter. A flower when opened before its time will not thrive. And though our belief in a life to come may be supported by such occasional glances caught in this life, it must

not take its foundation on them. A sound
and healthy belief is founded on arguments,
and it reaches to the highest points of view
of a healthy life, being itself essential to the
health and integrity of such a life.

Did you take the faint image in which a
dead person appears in your memory for a
mere inward semblance? If so, you have
mistaken it; it is more than that, it is your
friend's own self, consciously coming, not
only near you, but into you. His former
shape is still the garment of his soul, though
no longer encumbered with his former solid
body and wandering slowly along with him,
but transparent and light, free from earthly
burdens, changing its place in a moment, at
the call of every person who thinks of him,
or even entering into your mind of his own
accord, thus causing you to remember him
who is dead. The old idea, so generally
adopted, of the souls of the dead as light,
bodiless, unbounded by space, is quite a correct view of the subject, without earnestly
meaning to be so.

You have also heard of ghosts appearing—
what the doctors call illusions or hallucina-

tions. They are indeed hallucinations of the
living, but, at the same time, real manifestations of the dead. The faint images in our
memory are such manifestations, those vivid
apparitions are only the more so. It is no
use quarrelling whether they be one thing or
the other, for they are really both things at a
time. And as you are not frightened by the
images within you, being present manifestations of spirits, you need no more be frightened
by the apparitions before you. Though, after
all, in a certain sense, there is reason for being
frightened. The images of the memory are
either called up by yourself, or they come,
quietly and peacefully, in the course of your
inward life, as helps to its development ; the
other class of manifestations come unbidden,
too strong to be kept back, standing before
you it seems, but, in reality, standing within
you, not to help, but rather to disturb the
working of your inward life ; such a presence
is an abnormal one, belonging at the same
time to this life and the next. This is not
the way dead persons ought to hold intercourse with the living. To see dead persons
almost as distinctly and objectively as they

see each other, is almost death to the living; hence the fright of the living caused by their presence. And as, in those cases, the dead return half-way from the realms beyond the grave to the land this side the grave, popular belief—not an unfounded belief, perhaps— will have it that only such spirits walk forth and go about here as are not released yet, but still attached to this life with a heavy chain. To banish the unblessed spirit, call on the aid of a better and stronger one; but the best and strongest is the one Spirit above all spirits. In His protection, what can harm you? Popular belief agrees in this that evil spirits will vanish when the name of God is called upon.

There is, however, in this matter great danger of belief degenerating into superstition. The simplest means, after all, of keeping ghosts away is, not to believe in their coming. For believing that they may come is going to meet them half-way.

As the spirits see each other—I said above, meaning that such appearance, which is contrary to the order of things at present, is only anticipated from the order of things to

come.    Clearly, distinctly, objectively, the in-
habitants of the hereafter will see each other,
in the same shape of which we in this life
preserve but a faint likeness, a dim contour,
in our memory.    For they interpenetrate
each other with their whole nature, of which
a small portion only enters our minds when
we remember them.    In order to attract
them, it will be necessary to direct one's
attention towards them, in after-life as well as
at present.

Now you may ask, How is it possible for
those that interpenetrate each other to appear
to each other materially and in a distinct
shape ?    You may as well ask, How is it possible that that something which, in your
brain, produces the idea of a living person,
or the memory of a dead person (which is
all your mental property received from them),
appears to you as an outward object, or a
distant recollection.    The effects that produce your recollection have no distinct shape
themselves, yet they bring before you the distinct outlines of the person from whom those
effects went forth.    You cannot tell why it

is so, in this life ; how can you expect to know more of the hereafter ?

Thus, I say again, you must not draw inferences from supposed present causes unknown to you, nor from premises of your own invention; you must draw them from present facts known to you and all, and hence proceed to the greater and higher facts of the hereafter. One inference, by itself, may be faulty, so you must not stick to all the particulars; but the coincidence and accordance of all the different inferences, pointing towards that which is before and above all inference, will be the best support for your belief from below, and the best guide to the regions above. But if, from the beginning, you would take your footing above, the whole way that leads upward might slip from under your feet.

## CHAPTER XI.

THERE would be no more difficulties for our belief, could we only make up our minds to take the word that has been a fine saying for a thousand years and more, that " in God we live, and move, and have our being," for more than a word, or rhetorical phrase. In that case our belief in God and in our own eternal life would be one; we should look upon our own life as part of God's eternal life, and should consider the height of our future life above this present life as a higher step within God, from that lower step where we are placed in Him now; a better insight into the things below would enable us better to comprehend higher things, and from their mutual connexion we should comprehend the great whole of which we only form a part.

When your perceptions are gone out of your consciousness, recollections will rise out of them.  Thus your whole earthly *life of perceptions* will be gone one day, but a higher *life of recollections* will have risen out of it; and as your recollections move and associate within your head, the spirits of the hereafter move and associate within the Divine head. It is but a step higher on the same scale, which does not lead *to* God, but higher up *in* God, who holds within Himself top and bottom of that scale.  How empty must God appear to those who take the above-mentioned text for an empty sound; how full is God through the full meaning of those words !

Do you pretend to know how, in your present stage, a life of perceptions is possible in your mind ?  You know nothing but that there is such a life, which, being a spiritual life, is only possible in a spirit.  So there can be no difficulty for you to believe— although you know not how it is possible— that there will be a life hereafter, of your whole spirit in a higher spirit; if you only believe that there is a higher Spirit, and yourself in Him.

And again, there would be no more difficulties for our belief, if we could make up our minds to take for true that other word, that in everything God liveth, and moveth, and hath His being. Then there would be no dead world for us, but a living world, out of which every human being builds up his own future body, as a new house built up within the house of God.

When, oh when will that life-giving faith become alive among us ? The fact that it is a life-giving faith shall make it alive among us !

## CHAPTER XII.

YOUR question was, *whether* it would be; my answer is, *how* it will be. Belief renders your question as to the Whether unnecessary; but if the question is asked, there is that one answer as to the How. And as long as that How has not been settled, the Whether will not cease to come and go.

Here is the tree; let one or the other of its leaves drop away, if only its root be struck deeply and firmly in the ground: new branches and new leaves will grow and drop away again, but the tree will stand and bring forth blossoms of beauty, and instead of taking its root in belief, bear fruits of belief.

# APPENDIX.

VISION may be produced on several principles. If an opaque screen were placed in front of the retina with only a tiny opening in it, we could see through that opening, as every luminous point of the outer world would send a slender ray of light through it, and the rays crossing in the opening would produce an image, inverted, on the retina. But such vision by means of slender rays would be rather dim; that is not the way in which we see on earth. By another principle a pellucid lens is fastened in front of the retina to concentrate a whole cone of light, which issues from every luminous point of the outer world, into a point of the retina. This makes vision much more distinct; it is the actual principle of earthly vision, or rather of the outward process of it; for it does not explain the real act of seeing. For the soul does not see immediately the points of the image on the retina ; vision, as a mental act, is produced by the vibrations propagated into the brain, the different vibrations proceeding from one point being felt in one : whatever proceeds from a common source is perceived as one in the soul, though we cannot tell how a compound and extensive outward process is, as it were, condensed into a simple perception. It is, after all, natural enough for one and the same thing to afford a different appearance when seen from different points of view—one inward, the other outward— and it is a general experience concerning the connexion between body and soul that a simple psychological act rests on a physical complex, or, that the physically complicated is psychologically concentrated into something simple and one in itself. Vision may be explained through this law, and can hardly be explained differently, from the impossibility of proving a simple seat of the soul.

Now, a third principle of vision may be conceived, viz. the principle of interpenetra-

tion of the psycho-physical emanations (i. e.
physical processes producing psychical effects)
of two opposite points, the perception of
either point being produced in the other
immediately, by uniting those various emanations in one. And what holds good for two
points, would do for two systems of points.
This would be the most perfect vision, the
points of the objects appearing to each other
immediately and in their full intensity, in
proportion with the power produced by the
interpenetrating emanations, whereas in our
earthly vision it is not the points of the objects that are seen, only their images on the
retina.

I imagine that there could be a mode of
vision on this principle. The emanations of
celestial bodies, meeting each other in space,
do indeed correspond to it, supposing that
luminary vibrations, or concomitant vibrations of a higher order, may be considered
as psycho-physical movements (which suppo-
sition is nowise contrary to experience).
There has indeed always been an inclination
to connect our own mental life with movements of imponderable substance; nor can

there be anything to prevent our connecting such movements in the outer world with a mental life of a higher order. Even our human eye would not exactly require a lens in front of the retina to receive point-shaped impressions from outward points, if the retina itself, and each successive stratum of it, which now intercept outward emanations on their way to our psycho-physical system, should offer a surface of sensitive points to receive, and meet with their own emanations, directly and without any check or hindrance, the impression of the outward vibrations : as in the case of the luminary emanations of stars.

What is the good then of earthly eyes? It is this that in their connexion with our other senses, they help to form organs for effects of a higher order, organs which we call Men, who in their turn are connected, and united into an organism of a higher order than man, which we call Earth !

New vibrations go forth, no doubt, from the central points in which the fibres of the optic nerve terminate in the brain, vibrations propagated through the fibres between those points, and producing, where they meet, through the total of impressions caused by the single points, the perceptions of real objects : in the same way we may assume the perceptions of all the heavenly beings to be combined into a higher Divine perception.

Two naked men are evidently under the same outward conditions, reciprocally, as two stars ; however, they do not see each other with their skins ; for the psycho-physical system of man is inside him, closed up behind his skin, whereas that of the Earth is spread out over its surface, having its ultimate ramifications in the human beings that live on that surface. Now, there is one place in the skin affording an entrance to our psycho-physical system, namely, the eye, whereby men do indeed see each other. The rest of the emanations which they interchange, spread beyond them into the greater psycho-physical system, without affecting their own respective consciousness.

I am far from pretending that every point in this theory is well established, but I hope I have given a right idea of a right principle. It is no demonstration, it is only a remark, which I hope will prove the germ, still half-buried in darkness, to a great bright view of all things. My speculations, as laid down in this last and in the foregoing chapters, will become better established on larger and firmer grounds, and will be more generally adopted, when the science of psycho-physic, now only in its infancy, shall become aware that its subject is not an isolated theory of the relations between body and mind in the particular human and animal organisms, but a universal theory of the relations between the mental and the material principles of the universe. Such a time, of which this pretends to be a harbinger, shall come. To the materialist and the idealist my views must at present appear foolishness, just as the materialism and idealism of our days will one day appear foolishness in their turn.

FINIS.

LONDON:
PRINTED BY GILBERT AND RIVINGTON, LIMITED,
ST. JOHN'S SQUARE.

www.ingramcontent.com/pod-product-compliance
Lightning Source LLC
Chambersburg PA
CBHW020033030726
47499CB00007B/2400